The Crimson Crescent

This must be him, dressed in Arab costume and with thick streaks of dark brown make-up on his face! Disguised – and obviously up to no good! Lenny had the sick suspicion that something was terribly wrong. He even felt the word 'assassination' beginning to gather like a storm-cloud in his mind, and he might have shouted this word aloud as a warning, had not Sheikh Salami shouted first.

'The Crimson Crescent! It has disappeared!'

Also in Beaver by Hazel Townson

The Crimson Crescent

Hazel Townson

Illustrated by Philippe Dupasquier

Beaver Books

A Beaver Book

Published by Arrow Books Limited
62-65 Chandos Place, London WC2N 4NW

An imprint of Century Hutchinson Limited

London Melbourne Sydney Auckland
Johannesburg and agencies throughout
the world

First published by Andersen Press 1986

Beaver edition 1987

Text © Hazel Townson 1986

Illustrations © Anderson Press 1986

Made and printed in Great Britain by
Anchor Brendon Limited, Tiptree, Essex

ISBN 0 09 952110 5

Contents

For Derek Lomas and David Good, whose lectures sparked off my interest in children's books.

I

The Loathsome Lodger

'What's up with you?' Lenny Hargreaves asked his best friend, Jake Allen. 'You look as though you just got sentenced to ten years' non-stop school dinners.'

'My mum's taking a lodger.'

'What? With six kids and only four bedrooms?'

'I've got to move in with our Rod and Gary.'

'Help!' No wonder Jake looked so miserable.

As the eldest, he had always had a small room
to himself. Now he would have to share with
the three-year-old twins. The other three, all
girls, already shared a room.

'What does your mum want a lodger for?'

Jake shrugged. 'I suppose we just need the
money. My dad's firm can't give anybody a rise
this year 'cause business is bad.'

'Well, surely there's other ways of making
money besides turning your eldest son out of his
bedroom.'

'Go on, then; you suggest a few! And you can

spare us the fifty-pence-a-seat magic shows for
a start.' Jake had never been an admirer of
Lenny's conjuring repertoire, although Lenny
himself was determined to make a career of it
some day. All he needed was a bit more prac-
tice.

'I was thinking of your dad's job,' retorted
Lenny, feeling hurt. 'Maybe we could help him
get promoted.'

Jake's dad worked as a packing department
foreman at the local yoghurt factory, known as
Yummy Yoghurts Limited.

9

'Didn't you say old Spriggs, the manager, was due to retire at Christmas? All right then, what's to stop your dad from getting his job?'

'Plenty. There are three foremen, for a start, and my dad's the youngest. Anyway, it's no use him getting promoted if the factory closes down.'

'Gosh! Are things that bad? Still, it wouldn't close down if your dad was the manager. I'll bet he'd have some dynamic ideas that would really get things moving.'

'Such as?'

'I dunno—a new flavour, or something. Liquorice. That'd be a nice change.'

'Liquorice yoghurt?' Jake sounded thoroughly disgusted.

'I don't see why not. It's no dafter than cheese-and-onion crisps. If we went down to the factory every day after school and helped your dad, and gave him a few such ideas . . . ?'

'That's the best way I can think of to get him sacked. Then we'd all finish up sleeping on the kitchen floor and letting our upstairs out as a furnished flat.'

Lenny sighed with exasperation. It was very noble of him, he felt, to have offered up his precious free time, and Jake was a miserable, ungrateful wretch. At that point Lenny nearly gave up; let the Allens stew in their own juice! Yet Lenny's pride could not leave the problem unsolved. After more deliberations he said: 'All right then, we'll boost the whole business for 'em! We'll have an "Eat More Yoghurt" campaign. Then, when the factory's doing really well, everybody will get more wages.'

Jake still refused to cheer up. 'How do you think you'll manage that, then?'

'We could do a street survey, like they have at the elections. Excuse me, madam, did you know that yoghurt was the most health-giving food in the world, and that yaks in the Himalayas, who eat nothing but yoghurt, live to be two hundred and fifty years old?'

'Huh!'

'Failing that, my final suggestion is that you go and buy yourself a pair of earplugs so you can sleep through the racket your Gary and Rod will make. Plus a roll of barbed wire to keep them off your private possessions.'

It was this last sentence which brought home to Jake the full horror of his situation. In one icy premonition he saw exactly how life was going to be at home, and the best single word to describe it was 'unbearable'. As a drowning man will clutch at paper boats and soggy crisp bags, so Jake seized on Lenny's campaign. It was his only hope.

'All right then! I suppose we could chalk on the bus shelters "Yoghurt Rules OK" and stuff, if you think it will really do any good.'

'Chalking's a bit crude. You need to be a lot more subtle than that.'

'Well, that's my contribution, like it or lump it!'

'All right, keep your hair on! We'll go and get your chalks. At least it will stop you brooding.'

They started out for Jake's house, but as they rounded the corner of his street they saw a stranger with a suitcase turning in at Jake's garden gate.

'He's here already!' groaned Jake. 'And I

haven't even cleared out my wardrobe top.'

'Is *that* your lodger? Well, he looks as docile as a dolly-mixture. He won't stick it a week when he hears the racket you lot make.'

'He's paid a month's rent in advance. My mum's already spent it on new shoes for us all.'

'Oh, that's all right, then. I thought for a minute we weren't going to need our campaign after all. Just when I'd had some super ideas as well.'

'If you really want to know,' cried Jake in a great surge of frustration, 'I think yoghurt's horrible muck. Besides, most people round here have somebody in their family working at the Yummy factory. They're all sick to death of the thought of yoghurt.'

'Leave it to me!' grinned Lenny. 'By Sunday morning they'll all be begging for the stuff!'

2

The Powerful Poster

'Pleased to welcome you, Mr Orville.' Mrs Allen wiped her floury fingers on her apron before shaking the lodger's limp and sweaty hand. 'I hope you're going to be very happy here.'

Cassius Orville, glancing round the Allens' chaotic living-room, gave a sickly grin and gripped his suitcase even tighter.

'Here, let me take that and I'll show you to

your room.'

Mrs Allen held out a brawny arm for the suitcase. But the lodger had no intention of surrendering his property. Lifting it to his chest like a slumbering babe, he followed Mrs Allen up the stairs.

'Why's he called Mr Awful?' young Gary wanted to know.

'Just you keep on being your bright, cheeky self and you'll soon find out,' his eldest sister Julie warned him.

'And why's he got that funny brown lump on his cheek with all hairs sticking out of it?' asked Rod.

'That's a mole, and people with manners pretend they haven't noticed it,' said second sister Jill.

Rod was about to protest that moles had legs, but just then Jake and Lenny burst in. 'What's he like, then?'

'Harmless,' pronounced Julie confidently. 'He won't be any trouble.'

'Not to you,' grumbled Jake. 'He hasn't pinched your bedroom. Here, where are my chalks? I left them on the window-sill this morning.'

'Our Rod found them. He's crushed them up with his toy mallet. Serves you right for leaving your stuff all over the place.'

Jake swung his angry, frustrated face to Lenny. 'See what it's going to be like for me, sharing a room with those two? I'll go stark, raving bonkers.'

'Cheer up!' Lenny felt genuinely sorry for his friend. There were times when Lenny thought it a lonely business, being an only child; but this was not one of them. 'You'll just have to give in and join the main campaign.'

'*Now* what are they up to?' wondered Julie and Jill as the boys ran off.

'Haven't *you* any chalks?'

'No, but I've had a better idea. I've some felt-tipped pens I got for my birthday. I thought it was a soppy present at the time, but we could use them to make proper posters.'

Jake groaned. A quick chalked-up slogan was one thing, but a full-colour poster was another. It could take days.

'Haven't I told you? Everybody here knows about Yummy Yoghurts already. We'd be wasting our time.'

'Everybody knows about Guinness already, but they still keep advertising it. Anyway, I'm thinking of catching the visitors rather than the residents. We'll start with the Station Hotel. If we ask nicely at the desk they'll let us put a poster on their notice-board.'

Jake had grave doubts about this, but thought Lenny would find out soon enough. Let him work off his enthusiasm before it led to something even more drastic.

'What we could do with is some card or stiff paper.'

'I've got some white card in the top of my wardrobe. I saved it for making shields when we were supposed to be doing that Roman pageant that fell through.'

'Well, you go and get it, and I'll clear our kitchen table and sort out the pens.'

As Jake ran off home once more, he suddenly remembered that the sheets of white card were indeed still in the wardrobe, but that wardrobe now belonged to the new lodger. Jake's mother would have moved out his clothes and toys, but she wouldn't have bothered with a few sheets of card. She probably hadn't even noticed them. Jake almost turned back, then decided to go ahead and risk sneaking in for the card. If the lodger was downstairs, Jake could nip in to his old room unobserved.

As a matter of fact, Mrs Allen was giving Mr Orville a cup of tea and a meatpaste sandwich in the kitchen when Jake arrived. (Just as a first-day courtesy; she had no intention of making a habit of this.) However, it gave Jake just the chance he wanted. He sneaked upstairs, nipped into his old bedroom, opened the wardrobe door—and gasped with astonishment. There was a gun on the wardrobe shelf!

After a frozen moment of shock, Jake made a quick getaway, rescuing only the two bottom sheets of card, so that the lodger would not guess at the intrusion.

'Some docile dolly-mixture he turned out to be!' Jake thought he would burst with his exciting news long before he reached Lenny's

house. But Lenny took the information very calmly.

'He's got a gun; so what? He might have a dangerous job, like bank courier or all-night-bus driver.'

'He told my mum he worked in the Income Tax office.'

'Well, there you are, then! He needs it for self-defence. Anyway, ten to one it's only a dummy. They can look exactly like the real thing.' Lenny himself had a gun in his conjuring outfit. You fired it into the air and a load of feathers fell down—if you were lucky.

Guns held no mysteries for Lenny Hargreaves.

By now, Lenny was absorbed in roughing out his poster, and had even fetched a dictionary to look up how to spell yoghurt. He worked determinedly on, and turned out a bold and colourful piece of work. It showed a strong man standing on a giant Yummy Yoghurt carton, smiling broadly as he tied knots in a many-headed monster. At least, that's what Lenny said it showed. 'It's Hercules.'

'Looks more like a road accident to me,' sneered Jake. 'One smashed-up victim, three dead cats and a pile of debris.' Jake himself had

progressed no further than a wobbly, coloured border round the cockeyed letters: YOG.

Lenny chose to ignore both Jake's handiwork and his remark. Lovingly, Lenny gathered up his own poster and started off at once for the Station Hotel, with Jake trailing unhappily behind.

This was Cobston's largest establishment, frequented for the most part by dowdy commercial travellers and people who had got stranded overnight on the way to somewhere else. But any people were potential customers, Lenny told himself, and stranded travellers could eat yoghurt as well as the next man; better, probably, since travelling is supposed to make you hungry.

Lenny whizzed through the revolving doors and spun straight along to the reception desk, where a very nice blonde lady was hanging up keys on little hooks.

'Excuse me—please could you display this poster on your notice-board?'

The lady turned and stared at Lenny. 'Where did you spring from? Haven't you read the sign?'

Lenny hadn't; although it proclaimed in enormous letters: NO ADMITTANCE— CLOSED FOR TWO WEEKS.

'This is very important. You could be saving the town from terrible unemployment.'

'We're closed to the public until a week on Friday. We've got a private party in, so out you go, Bob-a-Job week or not!'

'No, you've got it wrong! What we're trying to do . . . ' Lenny began, but before he could say another word the hotel manager appeared.

'What seems to be the matter, Eunice?'

'I don't know how they got in, Mr Bliggins. I only turned my back for two seconds.'

'We got in through the door,' Lenny pointed out reasonably.

'Well, that's also the way out,' observed Mr Bliggins, grabbing Lenny by the back of his anorak and marching him in that direction. Lenny protested loudly, struggling to keep a foothold in the foyer until he had explained. Jake came loyally to the rescue. He and Lenny might have their differences, but they always

pulled together in a crisis.

'It may be only a poster, but it *is* important. It could save the yoghurt factory from having to close. If it does close, all the town will get poor, then nobody will want to stay in your hotel.'

Mr Bliggins turned quite pink in the face. 'You cheeky young scamp! Honestly, you kids these days—' He began a crescendo of indigna-

24

tion which would surely have ended in violence. But at the moment of almost-disaster a strange thing happened. A man in a very splendid Arab costume suddenly appeared in the foyer, snapped his fingers in the air and stopped Mr Bliggins in mid-phrase. Immediately, many more Arabs materialised—(though slightly less splendid than the first) until the whole hotel foyer took on the appearance of a scene from the Arabian Nights.

'What is happening?' asked the splendid Arab, whose name was Sheikh Salami. His voice was firm and resonant, accustomed to being obeyed. And since he had taken over the whole of the Station Hotel for a fortnight for himself and his entourage, he felt that he was entitled to obedience, explanations and anything else he might require. The fact that he was a multi-millionaire and one of the chief controllers of most of the world's oil supplies might also have had something to do with this feeling.

'Please do not disturb yourself, Your Highness,' spluttered Mr Bliggins. 'It's only a couple of kids—er, children—who have come to the wrong place by mistake.'

'No, we haven't,' Lenny spoke up boldly. 'We intended to come here because of the visitors.'

Sheikh Salami's eyebrows rose. 'Because of us?'

'Well, yes, if you're visitors. Though you don't look like the usual sort.'

Smiling, the Sheikh decided to explain. 'Your country makes many useful and beautiful things. We have come here to buy those things for *our* country. But we did not wish to stay in a noisy city. It is far more peaceful here.'

'Was!' corrected Mr Bliggins, a cold eye on Lenny, whom he still had not released.

Sheikh Salami raised his shoulders and spread his arms in a charming gesture. 'I know that I requested safety precautions, but a child—even two children—can do us no harm.' He beckoned Lenny and Jake towards him. 'Now, explain to me what you are doing here.'

'Well, you see, it's like this . . . .' Lenny began his story of the struggling yoghurt factory and his aim to improve its business prospects, though of course he made no mention of anything so personal as the Allens' lodger or their shortage of cash. Although Mr Bliggins grew fidgety, the Sheikh listened politely to every word, and neither he nor his countrymen moved until the story was finished. Then the Sheikh offered his thanks, patting both boys benevolently on the head. There was a moment's pause, then he said: 'I am truly amazed by this factory which has stirred up so much loyalty in such young children. I should like to see it.' His deep brown eyes stared down into Lenny's blue ones. 'Can you arrange for me a special visit to your factory? Shall we say—next Saturday morning?'

'No problem!' beamed Lenny, almost bursting at the seams with pride. Jake was not so sure (the factory was closed on Saturdays, for a start) but he did not want to spoil the moment of triumph. In any case, the Sheikh would probably change his mind before Saturday. Grown-ups were good at that.

'You boys will, of course, accompany me,' the Sheikh went on. 'Meet me here, at the Station Hotel, at ten hours. You will ride with me in my car.'

It was more of a royal command than an invitation.

So! Perhaps he did mean it after all—which left Jake wondering what his dad was going to say.

'Oh, boy!' cried Lenny when they were outside again. 'Is he rich? Did you see that whacking great jewel he was wearing—a solid ruby in a crescent shape, with diamonds like stars all round it?'

'I saw it! Couldn't miss it, could I? He's just a vulgar show-off. Anyway, I'll bet it's only Woolworth's.'

It took a while for the boys to discover that they had just set eyes on the Crimson Crescent, practically the most unique and priceless jewel in the world.

3
The Catastrophic Cough

To Jake's amazement, first his dad, then his dad's boss, Mr Spriggs, then the Managing Director of Yummy Yoghurts Limited, Mr Loftus himself, were all transported with delight at the prospect of Sheikh Salami's visit. Business was evidently looking up, for who knew what the wonderful outcome of such a visit might be? The Sheikh was reputed to have a household of one thousand persons, and if they could all be persuaded to eat yoghurt every breakfast time, the factory's troubles were over.

Mr Spriggs arranged double pay for the Saturday morning's overtime. Then he set most of the workers to cleaning, tidying and whitewashing the factory, whilst he himself went off to order an enormous new brass name-plate for his office door. As word went round the town, the dwellers in houses near the factory draped flags and bunting from their bedrooms, scrubbed their doorsteps and sold seats in their windows for at least a pound a time. It was to be the Sheikh's first public appearance in the town; an opportunity for folks to see whether the legends that had grown up around him were really true. (Did he honestly cover his toenails with genuine gold leaf, as Jenny Flounce, a chambermaid at the Station Hotel, had rumoured? And did he really carry a diamond-studded perfume-spray to keep at bay more ordinary odours?) The whole event began to assume the proportions of a major carnival.

As for Lenny and Jake, they felt like beings from another world as they arrived, well-scrubbed, well-groomed and well-lectured, for their ten o'clock Saturday appointment at the Station Hotel, there to behold, in all its splendour, the Sheikh's Rolls Royce motor car with tiger-skin rugs on the seats and a gold-plated telephone.

'We must be dreaming!' whispered Jake.

'It's real all right,' said Lenny, trying to sound as if he rode in a Rolls Royce motor car every day. 'I'm going to have one like this when I've got my own magic programme.'

Jake was too bemused even to scoff at this, and almost too bemused to unwrap his bubble-gum. He had vowed to give up ordinary chewing-gum after a terrifying time at the siege of Cobb Street School, but luckily bubble-gum (which was quite a different matter) had never been mentioned. Distractedly, Jake did at length pop a large pink slab into his mouth and began vigorously to torture it into shape. This helped his nervousness no end.

At last Sheikh Salami appeared, looking

even more splendid than before, and still wearing, Lenny noticed, the magnificent Crimson Crescent on his chest. The Sheikh's uniformed chauffeur, bearing an extra gold cushion or two, flung open the Rolls's rear door and Sheikh Salami climbed in, beckoning Lenny and Jake to follow. Lenny surreptitiously cleaned his shoes one by one on the legs of his best trousers, so as not to soil the fluffy white carpet within, and gave Jake a plainly disgusted look when he noticed him chewing. Oblivious, Jake settled himself by the window and the Rolls moved off, to be followed by a small procession of other cars. Cheers rang out as the resplendent motorcade approached the factory yard. The town had seen nothing like this since the Princess had come to open the new hospital, and everyone was determined to make a day of it. Cameras clicked and flashed; confetti flew and football rattles sounded. Jake and Lenny almost frizzled in the reflected glory, and Lenny decided then and there to wear a Sheikh's outfit for his first television 'magic' appearance. (Not only was it colourful

33

and dignified, but it had lots of useful, roomy folds.) Meantime, Lenny practised waving his hand and inclining his head like a visiting celebrity, while Jake blew surreptitious pink bubbles at familiar faces in the crowd.

Inside the factory there was no more than a semblance of normality. Work was certainly going on, but the workers kept bobbing up and

down to see what was happening and craning
their necks for a glimpse of the fabulous Sheikh.
Jake's dad was much in evidence, wearing a
blinding white overall which Mrs Allen had
bleached twice over for the occasion. He
walked back and forth with self-conscious
dignity alongside the conveyor-belt where
filled yoghurt cartons were deftly topped with

silver foil, then shuffled into boxes of ten before being borne away to the van-loading bay. Through a great mirror suspended overhead, Mr Allen could keep an eye on all parts of the room at once—or at least the workers were supposed to think he could.

The sight of the conveyor belt almost hypnotised Lenny, who thought that if he ever had to work there he'd turn dizzy in five minutes. It was interesting, though, especially trying to match up the different yoghurt colours with possible flavours. There was one which looked almost black, and Lenny wondered whether great minds had thought alike about the liquorice. How nice if they had, and it turned out to be a favourite flavour of the Sheikh's!

Lifting his eyes for a moment to escape the mad whirl, Lenny found himself staring through the overhead mirror, at the profile of one of the Sheikh's Arab retinue. The man was probably a bodyguard, since he kept his eyes intently on the Sheikh and one hand delicately fingering the air, as if ready to snatch, or push, or draw a weapon at the least sign of trouble.

Somehow, Lenny found this profile disturbingly familiar. Where had he seen it before? At the Station Hotel, most likely; and yet, the only Arab he felt he had really looked at there was Sheikh Salami himself. This face was different from the others. There was something not quite right about it. Puzzled, Lenny gave Jake an ill-aimed nudge to ask for his opinion. The nudge, which hit Jake at the back of the windpipe, started off an alarming coughing fit. The huge ball of bubble-gum which Jake had been enjoying suddenly shot from his mouth and landed in a passing yoghurt carton, which was immediately sealed by an inexorable metal arm and moved on before anyone else could have noticed.

A few seconds later, while Jake was still spluttering and gasping, Mr Loftus, the Managing Director, leaned forward, gathered up a newly-sealed yoghurt carton and offered it proudly to the Sheikh to taste. It was the very carton which contained the bubble-gum, though so far only Jake knew this. Until Mr Loftus had picked it up, Jake's horrified eyes had never left it.

The Sheikh beamed like a lighthouse—and Jake groaned like a foghorn. He had ruined everything!

4
The Violent Visitor

'Would you like to eat the yoghurt now?' Mr Loftus asked the Sheikh. 'I could send for a spoon from the canteen. We have some genuine silver spoons which we keep for distinguished visitors.'

But Sheikh Salami had already handed the carton to his aide, Mazrin, who walked just behind him at all times. The Sheikh would taste the yoghurt in the privacy of his hotel suite, he said. Just now he wanted to concentrate on the factory itself.

'I am wondering,' the Sheikh confessed to Mr Loftus, 'whether such a factory as this could be set up in my country. Your yoghurt looks so cool and smooth. If I find it enjoyable to eat, I shall come back to you for advice.'

Mr Loftus fairly danced with excitement. There would be no problem about setting up a branch abroad; he had often thought of it and wished for such an opportunity. Yoghurt would be just the thing for a hot, dry climate; soothing, refreshing, easy on the stomach . . . .

Jake Allen heard this conversation with a sinking heart. What a triumph this visit would have been, if only he hadn't gone and lost his bubble-gum! Now, disaster loomed! Once the Sheikh opened that yoghurt carton all was lost. Jake's dad would never forgive him (because Jake's mum would never let him) and Mr Loftus would never forgive Jake's dad. Jake would have liked to lie down and die.

By now, Lenny had noticed Jake's distress. Something was badly wrong, and he had better find out what it was. He drew his friend aside into a quiet corner, where Jake poured out his woeful tale in frantic whispers.

Lenny groaned and rolled his eyes. 'What am I always telling you? You and your blooming gum! One day your jaws will stick together, and serve you right!'

'I know,' admitted Jake penitently, 'but what are we going to do? If the Sheikh finds that bubble-gum he'll be so disgusted he'll never look at yoghurt again for the rest of his life. He'll probably ban it from his kingdom.'

'We'll have to get the carton back, of course.' Lenny became so taken up with the exercise of more ingenuity and the prospect of further adventures, that he forgot all about the teasingly familiar face he thought he had just seen. He began to breathe plans into Jake's ear. 'Just follow my lead, and everything will be all right.'

First, Lenny tried knocking 'accidentally' into Mazrin, the Sheikh's aide, hoping to make him lose his grip on the yoghurt carton. If he dropped it, Lenny, well-practised in sleight of

hand, would deftly substitute another carton and toss the offending one back on to the conveyor belt. But Mazrin had his feet firmly planted, was well-balanced and fully alert. He did not so much as wobble when Lenny pitched into his back with all the force of his five-stone-three.

'Oops! Sorry!' Lenny gave Mazrin a sickly grin which was not returned. Then Lenny had another idea. 'Would you like me to carry that for you?' Perhaps Mazrin was deaf, or maybe he didn't speak English. At any rate, his inscrutable face did not move the least muscle. He evidently did not share the Sheikh's paternal interest in the boys.

By now the party had come to the end of the conveyor belt, and Mr Loftus began steering everyone out of the room and along a corridor towards the loading bay.

'This is where our vans and lorries fill up and depart for all ends of the country,' he announced grandly, although just then there was only a single van in sight, and that had a puncture. Maybe this was the reason for Mr

Loftus's abrupt change of direction towards the canteen.

Lenny began to worry. If they started sitting around among the refreshments, the Sheikh might well decide to sample his yoghurt after all. The situation was growing desperate.

Lenny drew level with the Sheikh as they walked along. 'I'm training to be a magician,' he said. The Sheikh looked politely surprised.

'I'm going to have my own show on television one day. I already do little shows for kids' birthday parties and charity and stuff.'

'I, too, am fond of magic,' said the Sheikh at

last. 'Real magic, that turns a hot, dry desert into a thriving city. There is nothing to equal this.'

'Perhaps you'd like me to put on a little show for you? When we get to the canteen I could do a few tricks. My magic stuff's at home, but I could make do with a teatowel and a wooden spoon.' The Sheikh looked faintly interested and did not actually say no, so Lenny drew Jake aside once more and asked him to get hold of a box of ten yoghurt cartons from his dad. 'Tell him it's for the Sheikh and he's sure to give you one. I'll do my Zin-Zan-Zen—Multiply-by-ten trick, and we'll swap the box for that single yoghurt carton with your gum in it.'

Jake's eyes lit up. Filled with new hope, he turned immediately to find his dad. But at that very moment a strange scuffle erupted among the VIPs. Afterwards, nobody could quite describe properly what had happened, but it seemed as if one of the Arabs jostled the Sheikh, was jostled in turn by Mazrin, then staggered sideways into Jake, so that Jake fell over the Arab's feet with a deafening slap on to the concrete floor. The Arab, who had, thought Lenny, a curiously streaky face, then bent over to help Jake up. Everyone's attention was focused on Jake, who looked dusty and slightly dazed.

'You okay?' asked Lenny with some concern, though part of his mind was elsewhere. A few bits of puzzle had just clicked into place, for the Arab who had tripped Jake was the very one whose profile Lenny had previously thought familiar—and no wonder! Recalling that first glimpse in the mirror, Lenny realised that, besides very British features, the face had a mole on the left cheek, with hairs growing out of it. Cassius Orville had just such a mole—and a gun! This must be him, dressed in Arab costume and with thick streaks of dark brown make-up on his face! Disguised—and obviously up to no good! Lenny looked round to confirm his suspicions, but there were so many Arabs about, all wearing such similar clothes, that he could not spot his man. Nevertheless, Lenny had the sick suspicion that something was terribly wrong. He even felt the word 'assassination' beginning to gather like a storm-cloud in his mind, and he might have shouted this word aloud as a warning, had not Sheikh Salami shouted first.

'The Crimson Crescent! It has disappeared!'

This was followed by more words in his own language, causing instant pandemonium. Arabs began to seethe in all directions with a dignified, terrible speed. Yet Streaky-face had already disappeared.

5
The Chancy Chase

Lenny caught hold of Jake's arm and dragged him aside.

'You know who that was—that guy who tripped you up? It was your lodger, Mr Orville.'

'Oh, sure! And he was wearing my grandad's nightshirt.'

'I mean it! You couldn't mistake that great, hairy mole on his left cheek. And his face was all streaky. It was make-up! You said yourself he had a gun. Well, now we know what for. He came here meaning to steal the Crimson Crescent.'

'Have you gone bonkers, or what? It's not five minutes since you were calling him a docile dolly-mixture.'

'That's just an act he puts on, so nobody will suspect him. Only this time he overdid it. Nobody's *that* docile.'

'Well, for your information, Mr Orville's having a lie-in this morning. He even told my mum not to bother with any breakfast for him.'

'I'll bet he did! He wouldn't want her barging into his room with trays and stuff. You can't hide anything from your mum.' Indeed, as Lenny knew only too well, Mrs Allen's sharp eyes never missed a thing. At one and the same time she could dish up second helpings, catch a child stuffing unwanted cabbage down its sock, read her husband's newspaper backwards, smack a thieving hand away from the biscuits, wipe a child's nose and still observe that Lenny had bicycle oil all over his face. A formidable enemy!

'He's got away with it, too. He ran off while everyone was picking you up. I'll bet he's gone back to your house to change out of his Arab stuff and have a wash. Then he'll probably catch the next plane to Australia and live on his ill-gotten gains.'

Jake blinked. Sometimes he found it quite an effort to keep up with Lenny Hargreaves's imagination. But this time it looked as if Lenny could be right. There was certainly a hue and cry going on; the Crimson Crescent had undoubtedly disappeared; and if Cassius Orville hadn't taken it, then who had?

'We'd better tell my dad, then.'

Lenny sighed. 'Won't you ever learn? You don't honestly think your dad would believe a tale like that, do you? Or any other grown-up for that matter.'

'Well, we can't let him get away with it, lodger or not.' Jake was already dreaming of a triumphal return to his own room.

'We could follow him to your house. He thinks he's so clever, he'll never guess two kids have rumbled him. We could take him completely by surprise.'

'But suppose—?'

'No time! Come on!'

The boys started running towards the front door, but they didn't get far. A distraught Mr Loftus rose up before them with wildly waving arms, ordering every factory exit to be locked until the Crimson Crescent was found. The whole building must be searched, he said, and if that didn't produce the Crimson Crescent, then every person—workers, VIPs, the lot!—would have to be searched as well. (Except, of course, for the Sheikh and Mr Loftus himself.)

'That's done it!' groaned Lenny. 'Chase is off, then. We can't get out of here now.'

Then Jake had a brainwave. 'The doors might be locked, but there's still the chute,

where the boxes go down into the loading bay. It's too small for any grown-up, but we could squeeze through it with a bit of luck.'

'Well, what are we waiting for?' asked Lenny Hargreaves.

6

The Thwarted Theory

Emerging messily from the outside end of the chute, the boys began running all the way to the Allens' house. Bruised, battered and breathless they might be, but they were now even more determined to catch their criminal. Only one thing worried Jake, who was still having nightmares about his bubble-gum.

'Hey, I never got that box of ten yoghurts off my dad!'

'Plenty of time for that later. Once we've got the Sheikh's jewel back for him, he won't have the heart to refuse me a magic session.'

'But he could be opening that yoghurt this very minute.'

'Not him! He's not going to stand there scoffing yoghurt when he's just lost the most priceless jewel in the world.'

They arrived at the house just as Mrs Allen was returning from a major shopping expedition. One laden shopping trolley and two bulging carrier bags lay at her feet as she scrabbled impatiently in her purse for the front door key. Julie, the eldest girl, had her baby sister Joy in a push-chair and had evidently accompanied her mother, for the push-chair too was heaped with loaves and carrots and packets of detergent, which the baby was doing her best to chew to pulp, regardless of flavour.

Although trying his best to make a stealthy approach, Jake accidentally crashed the gate behind him.

'Be quiet, can't you? Mr Orville's still in bed.' Mrs Allen turned to admonish her son, then gasped with dismay. The two smart boys who had left together for their ten o'clock appointment at the Station Hotel had miraculously changed into two torn, crumpled, filthy ragamuffins. (That chute had been a good deal stickier and tighter than expected.)

'I don't believe this! I just don't believe it!'

'Come on, Mum! Unlock the door!' Jake hopped anxiously about. Even now, Mr Orville could be shinning down a drainpipe from a rear window, having changed back into his tax-inspector's suit.

'I'll give you "come on" when I get you inside! That was your only decent suit, and just look at the backs of your new shoes, all scuffed to cake-crumbs! That's the last time *you* get decent shoes, never mind what your dad says.'

Despite this outburst, Mrs Allen managed to open the door, hoist home the shopping, rescue the baby, pick up the milk and scoop three letters from the mat. Lenny did feel obliged to help, but Jake pushed rudely into the house, intent only on catching the thief.

And there Mr Orville was—staggering

sleepily down the stairs in his pyjamas and dressing-gown, hair rumpled and a newly-wakened daze on his face.

'What an actor!' thought Lenny with grudging admiration. 'And what a quick-change artist!'

'Sorry I'm so late up!' Cassius offered Mrs Allen a rueful grin.

'Never you mind! You're entitled to catch up with your sleep while you have the chance. I don't blame you. In fact, I wish one or two other folks had stayed in bed as well this morning.'

She cast a meaningful glance at Jake, who was already casting one at Lenny. Was there some mistake, Jake was wondering? It simply did not seem possible that Mr Orville could have done all the things Lenny had suggested, and yet be staggering around in his dressing-gown only half awake.

Lenny guessed what Jake was thinking, which was why he remarked very loudly: 'Hey, you've got a great, thick streak of brown make-up on your neck, Mr Orville!' The result of a too-hasty wash, was Lenny's implication, but Mrs Allen glanced at the lodger's neck and said oh yes, that brown cream she'd given him for his rash was doing a world of good. Then she turned to Jake.

'Upstairs right away! Get that suit off, and your old jeans back on! And change your shoes.'

'But Mum—!'

'Go on,' said Lenny, winking significantly. 'Do as your mum says. You do look a bit one-star.' He was trying his best to convey to Jake the inspiration to search Mr Orville's room for the cast-off Arab robes, not to mention the Crimson Crescent itself. If there were any hiding-places in that room, then Jake would know them.

Jake got the message, yet after a swift but thorough search he found nothing. What had Mr Orville done with those quite bulky clothes? Jake even looked in the dirty-laundry basket on the landing, and in the airing cupboard. What's more, he had once read a book where the thief had hidden his loot in a box hung on a rope outside his window, so Jake even checked there as well. That was when he spotted something which made his blood run cold. The 'Streaky-faced' Arab, who Lenny had thought was Mr Orville in disguise, was standing outside on the opposite pavement, staring up at the bedroom window!

7
The Anxious Arab

Mrs Allen's voice thundered upstairs.

'It's taking you long enough to change that suit. Has it fallen to bits, or what?'

'Our Rod and Gary have hidden my jeans!'

Jake, galvanised into action, left the window and changed as fast as he could. Panic had turned him into a fumbling, panting wreck, and it seemed to him as if he would never get back downstairs to Lenny. But at last Jake was able to drag his friend into the front room, out of earshot of the others, who by now were busy unpacking shopping and drinking coffee in the kitchen.

'You've got it all wrong! Streaky-face is outside. He's waiting for us! Honestly, Lenny, it gave me the creeps to see him standing there, looking up at the house.'

'What are you talking about?'

By the time Jake had explained afresh, and Lenny had argued (never finding it easy to be proved wrong), Mr Orville had eaten two thick slices of toast and had gone back upstairs to get dressed.

Lenny peered carefully round the front room curtain, and at last caught sight of the Arab standing patiently in the street.

'He followed us, then!'

Jake did not need to ask why. Streaky-face had realised that the boys had guessed his secret, and that maybe they could describe him. He must have come here to .... Jake's imagination, unlike Lenny's, had a sticking-point. He dared not let himself think too hard about what the Arab meant to do. Jake, in fact, was scared.

At that moment two things happened. Julie ran out of the back door on an errand for her mother, and the front doorbell rang. Jake grabbed Lenny's arm.

'It's him!'

'Well, he can't do anything to us while your mum's here. She'd soon sort him out.' Lenny had visions of Mrs Allen wielding a big, steel fish-slice, a weapon she had once used to threaten young Gary with when he stole a Mars bar from the corner toffee-shop. But Jake's mother was empty-handed when she went to answer the door.

The boys cowered silently in the front room, listening.

The Arab on the doorstep bowed politely. Sheikh Salami had sent him along, he said, to escort the two boys back to the factory right away.

'I thought the visit was over,' Mrs Allen said.

'Ah! But perhaps the boys have told you—there has been a little confusion.' Streaky-face went on to explain about the missing Crimson Crescent, and whilst he was doing so Lenny, with one eye round the edge of the front room door, was able to observe him more closely.

It was a chastening experience. This fellow *was* wearing make-up, and his features were definitely English, which was why Lenny had thought them familiar. But the mole was on his right cheek, not his left. Lenny had seen it through the mirror and forgotten to turn the image round. All right then; this man wasn't Mr Orville; but he was still no more an Arab than Lenny was, so Lenny's suspicions had not been entirely unfounded. As the man lifted his foot a step higher, Lenny could even see black shoes with stick-on soles, most un-Arabic footwear.

'Well, if there's all that fuss going on, the boys are best left out of it,' observed Mrs Allen with sound commonsense.

Streaky-face smiled again, a little less politely. 'But you see, it could all have been a simple misunderstanding. One boy fell down at the Sheikh's feet, and the Sheikh was wondering if

perhaps the Crimson Crescent could have slipped into the boy's pocket.'

So that was it! Lenny saw the whole plot at a glance. Streaky-face had stolen the Crimson Crescent then dropped it into Jake's pocket, either on purpose or by accident. Now he had come to claim it back.

'I can guess which boy fell down.' Mrs Allen called her son to the door. 'This one?'

Streaky-face agreed that it was.

'And you say he might have something in his jacket pocket?'

Streaky-face nodded slowly, staring with bewilderment at Jake's fresh outfit.

'Well then, you're a few minutes too late. I've just sent Jake's suit to the cleaner's. You should have seen the state of it!'

Now there was real panic in the Arab's eyes. He clutched at the sides of his head in a frenzy and glanced wildly round as if to spot the cleaner's. Jake was just as frenzied. To think he'd actually had the jewel in his possession and not known! And then, after all, for his mother to have done such a stupid thing! Would they ever see the Crimson Crescent again, or was it at this very moment dissolving in a pool of cleaning-fluid, or being crushed in a Hoffman presser? Jake would have dashed after the suit, which Julie had taken, but the next sensation was already happening. Lenny and Mr Orville had appeared in the doorway, and Mr Orville had a gun in his hand.

8

The Guiltless Gunman

All the time, despite his original flippant re-
marks, Lenny had kept the memory of Mr
Orville's gun at the back of his mind. As he
listened in to the doorstep conversation at the
Allens', he guessed that things could possibly
turn nasty, and decided to recruit the help of
the now undoubtedly innocent Mr Orville.

'But it's only a toy,' Mr Orville explained,
producing the gun at once when he heard

Lenny's breathless story. He had brought the gun along as a consolation present for the boy whose room he was taking over, but had decided Mrs Allen might not approve of the gift. So he had kept it in his wardrobe until he thought of something better.

'Never mind that,' said Lenny confidently. 'It looks real enough, and Streaky-face will never know. Just wave it around.'

'I can't go threatening people—'

'You don't need to threaten anybody. Just have the gun in your hand, and the criminal's conscience will do the trick.'

Lenny was absolutely right. Streaky-face took one look at the gun and fled, leaping on to a passing bus at the street corner. (He was never seen in Cobston again, although Lenny later spotted his picture in a national newspaper—dressed as a Red Indian this time—in connection with a missing tiara.)

'Now for my suit!' cried Jake. 'We'll have to hurry and grab it back before the cleaner does his worst.'

Mrs Allen sighed. 'Just come in, all of you, and shut that door! How daft do you think I am? I wouldn't send a suit to the cleaner's without going through all the pockets first. Is this what you're looking for?'

She dipped a hand into her overall pocket and drew forth a large, magnificent jewel which winked and sparkled in the gloomy hall.

'The Crimson Crescent!' breathed Lenny and Jake in chorus.

'Yes, well, you've quite a bit of explaining to do. In the first place, I want to know how you got hold of it.'

'Can we leave the explanations till later,

Mum? We have to take this back right away.'

'It's vital!' Lenny agreed. 'Sheikh Salami had got really interested in the factory until he lost this. Now, he's probably so fed up that he's ordered his lads to chop the place down with sabres.'

'He was going to give Yummy lots of business, and we'd all have been rich. So don't mess about, Mum!' Jake held out his hand for the jewel, but his mother dropped it back into her pocket.

'This thing must be worth a fortune. I'm not daft enough to let you go roaming the streets with it.'

'We roamed the streets with it before.'

'Yes, well, ignorance is bliss. Now that you do know what's going on, you can ring up your dad and tell him. Then your Sheikh can come and fetch his own property. Here's ten pence for the 'phone.'

Jake was horrified. 'You can't do that to a real Sheikh! You don't realise, Mum—he has a Rolls with tiger-skin rugs and a solid gold telephone—'

'In that case, it won't take him five minutes to get here.'

'But Mum, you can't ask him here!' Jake's outraged gaze took in the well-worn carpet strewn with toys, the child-high fingermarks along the walls and the line of nappies blowing in the back garden.

'Your mother's right,' Mr Orville butted in. 'It's not the sort of thing to be carrying about in your hand. It will be much safer in the house with your mother and me to look after it.'

'All right!' Lenny conceded temporary victory to the grown-ups. 'Come on, then, Jake. If we don't hurry up we won't even have the pleasure of telling where the Crimson Crescent is.'

'No further than that 'phone-box, mind, and straight back again. I'll be watching!'

'They won't believe us, Mum. You know what always happens if *we* tell a tale.'

'Well then, your Sheikh won't get his brooch back, will he?' Mrs Allen pinned the jewel to her jumper, then walked over to the mirror and admired herself, turning this way and that to

see the full effect.

'H'm!' she remarked at last. 'Can't see what all the fuss is about. I'd rather have a washing-up machine.'

Meantime, the boys crossed the street to the telephone box, but did not stop there. Whilst Mrs Allen was gazing into the mirror they ran defiantly on to the factory, only to find that the Sheikh and his party had already left.

'What a carry-on!' cried Mr Allen, who was busy locking up. 'First we heard this banging noise in one of the store-cupboards, so we opened it up and found this tied-up Arab in nothing but his underwear. Seems some villain had knocked him out and pinched his clothes, but he couldn't tell us who it was. Oooh, the Sheikh was blazing mad! He marched into his Rolls and sat there staring straight ahead without so much as a cheerio. And as for that stuck-up Mazrin, you know what *he* did? He was carrying that yoghurt carton that Mr Loftus had given the Sheikh, and he just dumped it in my hand as he sailed out, as much as to say, "You can keep your rotten yoghurt!"'

'Honest?' cried Jake, his face lighting up. 'What did you do with it, Dad?'

'I showed him! It wasn't his to chuck away. I dumped it right back again on the seat next to the Sheikh's chauffeur. Only just in time, as well. He nearly took my hand off when he slammed the door.'

Jake felt he had just aged about twenty years, but Lenny, business-like as ever, demanded crisply: 'Well, just a minute before you lock up, Mr Allen! We need a box of ten yoghurts right away. You'll have to trust us for the money, but if the worst comes to the worst I've got four pounds sixty saved up for a new

73

magic trick.'

'Don't tell me you've suddenly got a craving for the stuff? I thought the only things you two liked to get your teeth into were toffee, ice-cream and bubble-gum.'

9
A Fitting Finale

All that was visible in the foyer of the Station Hotel was the blonde head of Eunice bowed over a ledger. Lenny stepped confidently into the revolving door, having noted that the NO ADMITTANCE sign was still in place.

Hearing the hiss of movement, Eunice looked up.

'Oh, no! Not you two again!'

'It's really important this time,' Lenny

began. 'We've actually found . . . .'

'I don't know what you've been up to,' interrupted Eunice, pointing rudely with her pen, 'but until you turned up the Sheikh was very happy here. Polite and charming all the time, he was; a perfect gentleman. But since he came back from that factory he's been carrying on something shocking, and now he says he's leaving, though he'd booked in until next Friday.' (Eunice was, in fact, just adding up the bill.) 'So you'd better not let Mr Bliggins catch you here, that's all!'

Too late! Mr Bliggins had already materialised from the direction of the lift. His wrath assumed new dimensions. When he began to speak, it was as if there were several voices inside him, all struggling to be first out. Lenny and Jake could not identify a definite command, so they just stood there letting the words pile up like bomb debris around them. The onslaught did not last long. As before, it was interrupted by the sudden appearance of Sheikh Salami and company, though this time the Sheikh's manner was as cold and hard as a lump of frozen flint. He gave no greeting, but stared unsmilingly down at Lenny, who drew breath for his big moment. But Jake beat him to it. 'We've found your Crimson Crescent!' he blurted out.

Since the boys could not produce the jewel, the Sheikh's frosty manner did not even begin to thaw. It was doubtful whether the boys would ever have persuaded him to drive to the Allens' house to collect his property. Fortunately, they didn't have to, for whilst they were talking Mr Allen walked in with the Crimson Crescent wrapped in cotton wool inside an empty tea-packet.

'Your mother didn't mind *me* getting mugged,' Jake's dad grinned. 'Sent me off with it as soon as I opened the door.'

Of course, the Sheikh was now overjoyed, and ordered refreshments to be sent up to his suite at once.

'You must be my guests,' he told Mr Allen and the boys. 'Besides, I believe we have a magical appointment still to keep?'

Lenny Hargreaves had spotted the yoghurt carton on the table as soon as he walked into the suite, and could have wept with relief to see it still intact. Now, at the Sheikh's command, he moved to the table for the most vital performance of his career.

Clearing away all but the carton, he set this in the exact centre of the table. Then he took from his bag a magic baton and a bulky black cloth which seemed heavier than it ought to be.

'Don't look till I get everything sorted out.'

At last he was ready. He arranged the black cloth carefully over the single yoghurt carton and waved his baton.

'Zin, Zan, Zen, multiply by ten!'

Then he whipped away the cloth, to reveal a box of ten yoghurts sitting snugly in the middle of the table. Sheikh Salami laughed delightedly.

'But you have multiplied by eleven!'

It was true! Lenny had forgotten to whisk away the original carton, which the Sheikh now gathered up.

'That was very good magic. But now I shall

try for myself the magic taste.' He began to peel away the silver foil.

'No!' cried Jake, but it was too late. The Sheikh had already taken a spoon and dipped it in.

'But he finished it all, so where was the bubble-gum?' Jake asked Lenny afterwards.

'He must have eaten it.'

'Will he die?'

'Dunno! We'll just have to wait and see.'

They waited three long, anxious days—until they discovered that Mr Loftus was even better at sleight of hand than Lenny Hargreaves. For Mr Loftus, too, had seen what happened at that fateful coughing fit, had deftly grabbed the ruined carton, slipped it into his pocket and just as deftly substituted another to offer to the Sheikh. Since then, he had had a perspex cover fitted over the conveyor belt so that no such disaster could ever occur again.

That had been a nasty moment! It was just as well that Mr Loftus had no more time to think about it. He was far too busy with plans for the building of the first foreign factory of Yummy Salami Enterprises Limited, which Cassius Orville, sick of taxes (both other people's and his own) had already gone off to supervise.